The New Adventures of
MARY-KATE & ASHLEY™

The Case Of The
Wild Wolf River

D1042550

The Case Of The

Wild Wolf River

by Judy Katschke

DUALSTAR PUBLICATIONS PARACHUTE PRESS

SCHOLASTIC INC.

New York   Toronto   London   Auckland   Sydney

DUALSTAR PUBLICATIONS   PARACHUTE PRESS

Dualstar Publications
c/o Thorne and Company
1801 Century Park East
Los Angeles, CA 90067

Parachute Press
156 Fifth Avenue
Suite 325
New York, NY 10010

Published by Scholastic Inc.

With special thanks to Robert Thorne and Harold Weitzberg.

Printed in the U.S.A.
August 1998
ISBN: 0-590-29401-6
E F G H I J

1

MONTANA, HERE WE COME!

"**M**ary-Kate," Ashley cried. "You can't make the phone ring by staring at it!"

I kept looking at the phone on my desk. "Maybe it will work if I don't blink," I said.

My twin sister, Ashley, and I were in the attic of our house in California. That's where we run the Olsen and Olsen Mystery Agency. Business is usually great, but it's been really slow ever since school ended.

"Let's face it, Mary-Kate," Ashley said. "It's the middle of the summer. Nothing is going on.

Most people are on vacation."

"We haven't solved a new mystery in over a week!" I tapped my fingers on the desk. "What are we going to do all summer if we can't solve mysteries?"

Ashley sat down at her desk. "We can…go to the beach," she suggested.

"The beach?" I jumped up. "Yeah! Maybe we'll find some jewels buried in the sand. We can figure out who hid them there! Or maybe there's a secret cave hidden in the bluffs, and—"

"Or maybe we can just swim," Ashley interrupted me.

"I never thought of *that*," I joked. I love swimming as much as Ashley does. But most of all, I love solving mysteries!

Clue, our basset hound, came running into the attic. Clue is the silent partner in our detective agency. She has a real nose for sniffing out important clues.

"Wait a minute! What's that soggy thing in

Clue's mouth?" Ashley asked.

"Your scrunchie," I said. "I didn't want Clue's detective skills to get rusty. So I had her sniff your hairbrush and then I told her to follow the scent to your scrunchie!"

"Gross!" Ashley took the scrunchie from Clue's mouth. "Mary-Kate, you have to be patient," she went on. "Who knows? Our best case ever might be just around the corner!"

"That's easy for *you* to say." I sighed.

Ashley and I may look alike, but we think in different ways. If you could see our thoughts, Ashley's would be straight lines. Mine would be zigzags and squiggles! She's always sensible and patient. But I like to charge right into things.

R-r-r-ring!

I grabbed the phone so fast, I bumped my elbow on the desk.

"Ouch!" I yelped into the phone. "Oops! I mean, Olsen and Olsen. Can we help you?"

"You can come with me to the beach!" a

voice said. "It's too hot to stay inside!"

It was our friend Samantha Samuels.

"Sorry, Samantha," I said. "But we can't close our mystery agency to go to the beach."

Ashley's eyes grew wide. She snatched up the phone on her desk. "Oh, yes, we can!" she told Samantha. "We'll meet you at the beach in an hour. Next to the ice cream stand."

"But, Ashley," I said after we hung up. "What if somebody calls with the biggest mystery in the world while we're tossing Frisbees at the beach?"

"Then whoever it is will call again," Ashley said. "Come on—don't you want to jump into the nice, cold water? Wiggle your toes in the sand? Eat an ice cold slushie…with cherry syrup?"

I leaned back in my chair and closed my eyes. It *was* hot. And that cherry slushie sounded great.

"Okay," I said. "Let's put on our swimsuits."

"Great!" Ashley jumped up and ran toward

the stairs. I started to follow her, but then the phone rang again.

"It's probably Samantha," I said. I picked up the receiver. "Don't worry. We'll bring our boogie boards," I said.

"What's a boogie board?" a boy asked.

I didn't recognize his voice. "Who is this?" I asked.

"This is Jason White Eagle," he said. "Is this the Olsen and Olsen Mystery Agency...home of the famous Trenchcoat Twins?"

"This is the Trenchcoat Twins...well, one of them," I said. "I'm Mary-Kate Olsen. How did you hear of us?"

"I read about you in *Kool-Kidz* magazine," Jason explained. "You're supposed to be awesome detectives—and I need a mystery solved."

Yes! A mystery! I pumped a fist into the air.

"What's the mystery?" I asked, excited.

"I live on my grandpa Joe's ranch in Montana," Jason answered. "We're Native

Americans of the Blackfoot tribe. Grandpa has a collection of valuable crafts. And they're disappearing one by one!"

"That's awful," I said. "What kind of valuable crafts?"

"A beaded tribal necklace, a feathered headdress, a drum, and a wooden carving of a wolf," Jason explained. "The first members of our tribe made these crafts hundreds of years ago. Then they were passed down from family to family. Now they belong to my grandpa— except he doesn't have most of them anymore. They've been stolen. Can you help us?"

"We'll be there tomorrow," I answered.

I hung up the phone and glanced at our map of the United States. Montana was all the way at the top of the country.

"Ashley!" I cried. "We'd better get packed. Our next case is in *Montana*!"

The Trenchcoat Twins were back in business!

2

STOLEN TREASURES

"**A**re you sure this is the same sky we have in California?" Ashley asked Jason and his grandpa. We had just arrived at the White Eagle Ranch.

Grandpa Joe laughed. "That's why we call Montana 'Big Sky Country.'"

"Big Sky Country," I repeated. "I like it here."

Jason pointed to Clue. "I think your dog likes it here, too," he said. "Her tail hasn't stopped wagging once!"

Clue barked. She wore a red bandanna around her neck. Ashley and I were also dressed for the ranch, in jeans and plaid shirts.

"You'll be staying at the main house," Jason said. "But I'll show you around the ranch first."

Ashley frowned. I knew just what she was thinking. "It looks kind of big," I said. "I might need my hiking boots if we're going to walk around the whole ranch."

"The White Eagle Ranch is much too large for walking," Grandpa Joe said. He put his fingers in his mouth and whistled. A minute later, two ranch hands came over leading three beautiful horses.

"Meet Butterscotch, Tumbleweed, and Cloud," Grandpa Joe said.

"Cloud is my horse," Jason told us proudly.

"I *love* to ride horses," I cried.

"I'm still a beginner," Ashley said nervously.

"Then you take Tumbleweed," Jason suggested. "She's as gentle as a lamb."

"What about Clue?" Ashley asked.

"No problem," Jason said. He patted a basket attached to Cloud's saddle. "Clue can ride in here."

"I'll take your suitcases back to the main house," Grandpa Joe said with a wave.

Ashley turned to me. "Do you have your tape recorder?"

"Check," I said. "Do you have your notebook?"

"Check," Ashley replied. "We're ready to start our case!"

The tape recorder and the notebook were gifts from our great-grandma Olive. She used to read us all these neat mystery stories, until we decided to solve mysteries ourselves. And Great-Grandma Olive told us that a good detective is always prepared. That's why Ashley and I never go anywhere without our detective equipment.

"This part of Montana is called the 'Great Plains,'" Jason told us as we rode. "The land is flat—it's perfect for raising cattle." He pointed to a fenced-in pen. "That's our corral."

Ashley and I stared at the corral.

"There must be a hundred cows in there!" Ashley said. "I guess you never run out of milk for your cereal, Jason."

"Those aren't cows." Jason laughed. "Those are bulls!"

"Whoops!" I said. "I guess we're not very good cowgirls...yet."

"But we *are* good detectives!" Ashley reminded me. She turned to Jason. "So tell us more about your mystery."

"Well, not many people have *real* crafts made by the Blackfoot Indians," Jason said proudly. "Grandpa Joe liked to share them with our guests. Our ranch is also a hotel. Grandpa Joe displayed the artifacts in the main house, and people from all over the country used to come to see them."

"*Used* to come?" Ashley asked.

"The headdress, drum, and necklace are

gone," Jason said sadly. "The only thing left is the wolf carving...until someone tries to steal that, too."

"Are you sure someone stole them?" I asked. "Maybe they're just lost."

Jason shrugged. "Grandpa Joe kept them in a special room in the main house. Nobody ever moved them, so they couldn't have gotten lost."

Ashley pulled her detective notebook out of her pocket and began writing down what Jason said.

"We called the sheriff," Jason went on. "He looked around. But he said it didn't appear as if anyone broke into the house. And he checked for fingerprints, but he didn't find any."

"Did someone always watch the crafts when guests came to look at them?" Ashley asked. "And do you keep your house locked at night?"

"Always!" Jason answered both of Ashley's

questions at one time.

"Now, *that's* what I call a mystery!" I said.

Ashley nodded. "*That's* why we're here!"

We rode past a group of small houses made of wood. A bunch of kids played tag in a yard. One man was starting up a barbecue.

"The ranch hands and their families live here," Jason said.

"Could any of them be suspects?" I asked.

Jason shook his head. "They were all questioned and cleared by the sheriff."

"Good," Ashley said. "They look so nice."

Two kids waved to us.

"Everyone is happy to have the Trenchcoat Twins on the case," Jason said. "You guys are famous!"

But as we turned our horses toward the main house, I noticed a big piece of yellow paper tacked to a fence. I rode Butterscotch closer and tilted my head to read it.

"Uh-oh," I said. "I don't think *everyone* is happy we're here."

"Why not, Mary-Kate?" Ashley asked.

I pointed to the note.

Written on it in big black letters were the words: TRENCHCOAT TWINS, GO HOME— OR YOUR LIVES WILL BE IN DANGER!!

MYSTERY GUESTS

"**I**t's a threat," Ashley said with a gulp. "But why would anyone want us to go away?"

I yanked the note off the fence. "I can think of only one person who would want us to leave—the thief. So that must mean whoever wrote this note is the thief!"

Ashley nodded. "That note is our first clue," she said. She rolled up the paper and slipped it into the basket with Clue.

"Well, we're *not* going home," I said. "So the thief better watch out!"

Jason gave us the thumbs-up sign. "Way to go, sleuths!"

I pulled out my mini-tape recorder and spoke into it.

"July twenty-second. Eleven-thirty A.M. White Eagle Ranch, Montana. Clue Number One: Creepy note. Possibly written by—" I heard the thunder of hooves. I switched off my tape recorder and whirled around. A boy with spiky hair charged toward us on a black horse.

He stopped his horse so close to us that its hooves kicked up dust—right into our faces!

I sneezed. So did Butterscotch.

The boy looked down his nose at Ashley and me. "Are you the Trenchcoat Twins?"

"That's us!" Ashley said.

"Then why aren't you wearing *trench-coats*?" he asked.

Ashley shrugged. "We left our coats at home."

The boy rolled his eyes. "Maybe you left your detective brains at home, too."

Ashley gasped.

I looked over at Jason. Did he *know* this guy?

Jason sighed. "I'd like to apologize for my friend, Weasel Coleman," he said.

"Weasel?" I repeated.

"My real name is Mike, but I like Weasel," he said. "Weasels are fast. Weasels are smart. Weasels are—"

"A little mean!" Ashley interrupted.

Weasel grinned. But it wasn't a friendly grin—it was a nasty one.

We rode toward the main house. Weasel followed us.

"So who do you think stole the crafts?" Weasel called from his horse.

"We don't know yet," Ashley said. "We just got here."

"A good detective would have about *ten* suspects already!" Weasel scoffed.

Jason leaned over and whispered to me. "Weasel is always reading mystery books and renting spy videos. He thinks he knows every-thing about mysteries!"

"Well, he doesn't know everything about *us*!" I whispered back. "We've never had a case we couldn't solve."

We stopped our horses in front of the main house. The outside was painted white with dark green shutters. There was a porch up front, filled with wicker rocking chairs.

"What a great house!" I said.

A long, shiny black car was parked in the driveway. Just as we started to climb down from our horses, a chauffeur opened the back door of the car and two people stepped out.

The first one was a woman. She wore a yel-low dress, lots and lots of gold jewelry, and a straw cowboy hat. The other one, a man, had on a white suit. He wore a cowboy hat, too...but they sure didn't look like cowboys!

"Who are *they*?" I asked.

"That's Emily and Henry Bixby. They own dozens of buildings in New York City," Jason told us. "That's where they live."

"Aren't you two supposed to know things like that?" Weasel asked. "What kind of detectives are you, anyway?"

I didn't bother to answer him.

Ashley stared at the woman's jewelry. "I thought she looked rich," she said. "What are they doing here?"

"The Bixbys stay at the ranch one weekend every month," Jason said. "They say they like to get away from the big city."

Ashley and I glanced at each other. This could be another clue! "Do they stay in the main house?" Ashley asked.

"Are you kidding?" Weasel laughed. "The Bixbys stay in the private guest house. With two whole bathrooms!"

Jason laughed. "And their dog, Cinnamon, drinks spring water from a crystal dish!"

A little brown Chihuahua peeked out of Emily's dress pocket. Clue must have seen him, too, because she barked softly.

"Oh!" Ashley said. "Look how cute!"

"Cute?" Weasel cried. "He's an ankle-biting rat!"

The Bixbys strutted past us without saying hello.

"They don't seem very friendly," I whispered to Jason.

Grandpa Joe stepped out on the porch. "Henry! Emily!" he called. "Welcome back. I hope your stay will be pleasant!"

Henry tipped the brim of his hat. "It'll be a lot more pleasant if you agree to sell us your wolf carving," he said.

Grandpa Joe smiled and shook his head. "I'm afraid I haven't changed my mind."

When the Bixbys went inside, I turned to Jason. "What was that all about?" I asked.

"Every time the Bixbys visit, they try to buy my grandpa's crafts," Jason explained. "For tons and tons of money!"

"Did your grandpa ever sell them *anything*?" Ashley asked.

Jason shook his head. "No! Grandpa Joe wouldn't sell those artifacts for all the money in the world. That is…what's *left* of them."

Ashley smiled at me. I knew what she was thinking, because I was thinking exactly the same thing! Emily and Henry Bixby were suspects #1 and #2!

"Do you think *they* could have left that note for us?" Ashley asked.

"Well, we don't know *exactly* when they got here," I thought out loud. "They could have heard we were coming. And they could have put it there before we arrived."

"We'll definitely need to do more investigating," Ashley said.

"Jason? Did the Bixbys stay at the ranch on the days that the crafts were stolen?" I asked.

"I'm not sure," he answered.

"When people make reservations to stay here, does your grandpa write it down?" Ashley asked.

Jason's eyes lit up. "Yeah—he writes the

names on his calendar. We can check it out!"

We tied our horses to a row of hitching posts. Jason helped Clue out of the basket. Then we hurried into the main house.

"The Bixbys always drink iced tea in the living room when they get here," Jason whispered. "So let's go to my grandpa's office right now."

We tiptoed past the living room into Grandpa Joe's office. We ran straight to a huge calendar hanging on the wall. Weasel followed us.

Jason flipped back the pages.

"The Bixbys started coming about four months ago," Jason said. He pointed to the dates. "See? This is when they stayed here in June…and in May…in April…and in March."

Ashley wrote down each date in her book. Then she showed it to Jason. "Are these the same days that the artifacts were stolen?" she asked.

"Well, none of the crafts disappeared in

March...." Jason's eyes opened wide. "But those other days were definitely the days when the crafts were taken! I'll never forget those horrible days."

I snapped my fingers. "Ah-ha! Then the Bixbys must be the thieves! Maybe they came in March, saw your family treasures, and decided to start stealing them the next month."

Ashley shook her head. "Other people stayed at the ranch on those days, too, Mary-Kate. We have to think of all possible suspects," she said.

"You're right," I admitted. "But they were here exactly when the things were stolen."

"I know," Ashley said. "But remember what Great Grandma Olive taught us—don't jump to conclusions."

I frowned. This case was getting complicated. "Let me see that calendar," I said. I reached around Jason and turned the pages one by one. Then I noticed something!

"Hey," I said. "There's a little black circle on each date that the crafts were stolen. What do they mean?"

"I don't have any idea," Jason said.

"I know!" Ashley cried. "My pocket calendar has those black circles, too. They're symbols. For when the moon is full!"

"Which means," I said slowly, "that the crafts disappeared on the nights of the full moon."

"That's the best clue yet!" Jason cried. He looked at Weasel. "I told you they were good detectives!"

Weasel snorted. "Anybody could have figured *that* out," he muttered.

I stared at the calendar. "Uh-oh. We're going to have to be *really* good detectives now," I said. "Because the next full moon is tomorrow night."

"Which means," Ashley added, "that the thief might strike again!"

4

FULL MOON...TOO SOON!

"That hardly gives us *any* time!" I groaned.

Weasel laughed. "That's because it will probably take you ten years to solve this case. If you solve it at all!"

I wanted to step on Weasel's toe—hard. But I decided to ignore him instead.

"Show us where your grandpa keeps the crafts," I told Jason. "We have to start looking for more clues right away."

Jason led us down a hall to a small room. Inside was a colorful rug, two chairs, and a gigantic glass display case.

"The necklace and the drum were kept inside this glass case," Jason said. "And the headdress used to hang on the wall between the chairs."

Jason pointed to the corner of the room. "As you can see, the wolf carving is the only thing left."

Ashley and I turned to look at the wood carving. It showed a wolf howling up at the sky. "That must be at least five feet tall!" I said.

"What did the other crafts look like?" Ashley asked.

Jason showed us a wall covered with framed photographs. One was a picture of a man wearing a huge feathered headress.

"That's my great-grandfather," Jason explained. "He used to wear the headress at special ceremonies."

Ashley pulled out her notebook and began taking notes. "Is this the missing drum?" she asked, pointing at another photo.

"Yeah," Jason said. "If you look closely, you can see that the drum was trimmed with feathers and tiny silver bells."

I stared into the glass display case. It was empty except for a large photo. This one showed a woman. Around her neck was a necklace made from large, smooth stones beaded together.

"That was my great-grandmother wearing the missing tribal necklace," Jason told me.

"The necklace is the only thing that's small enough to carry easily," I said thoughtfully. "You'd have to be pretty strong to carry that big drum."

"Or the headdress," Ashley added. "That thing is so huge that if I put it on my head, I'd fall right over!"

"No wonder the thief came back three times," I said. "He or she probably couldn't carry everything out at once."

I searched the room for clues. Ashley looked for fingerprints on the glass display case. Clue sniffed the rug. But we didn't find anything.

I took out my mini-tape recorder.

"You call that thing spy material?" Weasel asked. "I have a tape recorder much smaller than that!"

I held the tape recorder to my mouth and pressed the on button. "Zero clues around the glass display case," I reported.

"Maybe you can't work without your trenchcoats!" Weasel snickered.

I was getting really sick of Weasel teasing us. I opened my mouth to tell him off, but just then a woman with short black hair came into the room with Grandpa Joe.

"Or maybe they can't work on an empty stomach," the woman said with a smile. "Lunch is just about ready, kids."

"This is my mom," Jason told us.

"Nice to meet you, Mrs. White Eagle," I said.

"We were just looking at the wolf carving,"

Ashley said. "It's *so* beautiful!"

Grandpa Joe walked over to the big carving. "The wolf always has had special meaning to the Blackfoot people."

"Why is the wolf so important?" I asked.

"Many years ago, hunters disguised themselves with wolf skins when they hunted buffalo," Grandpa Joe explained. "Since the buffalo were much larger than the wolves, they weren't afraid of them. So the hunters could creep up on the buffalo without scaring them away."

"The wooden wolf was carved by someone in our family hundreds of years ago," Mrs. White Eagle said. "It was meant to bring us luck in the hunt. And since wolves are thought to be very smart, it was also supposed to bring us wisdom."

"That's why it's important to me," Jason joked. "I need it for help on my math tests!"

Grandpa Joe gently placed his hand on the wolf's head.

"If this wolf is stolen," he said softly. "We'll lose a lot more than just a carving. We'll lose a part of our tradition."

"Don't worry, Grandpa Joe," I said. "We won't let anyone steal it, and we'll get your crafts back, too!"

"Maybe we can start by talking to people who live in town," Ashley suggested.

Grandpa Joe winked at Jason. "Then I think it's time for you girls to meet the wild wolf!" he said.

Ashley and I stared at each other.

"Um...wolves might be smart, Grandpa Joe," I said slowly. "But I'm not sure I want to meet one."

Grandpa Joe laughed. "I meant the Wild Wolf River. It leads straight to town!"

Jason's eyes were shining. "We can raft down the river. It's the fastest way to go!"

"Jason is an experienced rafter," Mrs. White Eagle explained. "He's taken many people out on the river."

Ashley and I had never been rafting before. I was so excited, I could hardly speak!

"Can Clue come?" I asked.

"Sure!" Jason said. "All the dogs I know love riding in rafts."

"I'm coming, too," Weasel insisted.

Ashley rolled her eyes. "Great," she whispered to me.

I knew just how she felt. I was getting the idea that Weasel planned to follow us all weekend!

After lunch, Ashley and I followed Jason and Weasel to the river.

"What's that whooshing noise?" I asked as we walked.

"That's the Wild Wolf," Jason explained. "You can't see it yet, but you can sure hear it!"

The boys led us through a clump of trees.

"Ta-daaaaa! The Wild Wolf River!" Jason said proudly.

The river was so wide, I could barely see

the other side! The sun sparkled on the white, bubbly water. Smooth, wet stones peeked out like shiny turtles.

"It's awesome," I said. Ashley and I slapped a high-five.

"You'd think they'd never seen a river before," Weasel said.

"We have, but not like *this*!" Ashley admitted.

"There's the raft," Jason said. He pointed to a big rubber raft. It was filled with helmets and paddles.

Jason began walking down the riverbank.

"Be careful," he called over his shoulder. "The mud can be pretty slippery."

Ashley turned to me and shook my arm. "This is going to be *soooo* cool!" she cried.

"I know," I said. I pointed down at her foot. "But you'd better tie your sneaker first."

Ashley knelt on the muddy ground to tie her sneaker. "I wonder what this is?" she asked, staring at the ground.

"It's mud," Weasel said. "You know—wet dirt." He snickered.

"What is it, Ashley?" I asked, ignoring Weasel.

"Something stuck in the mud," she said. "Something shiny."

I watched Ashley as she dug her fingers into the mud—and pulled out a small piece of silver. She picked it up and stared at it for a minute.

"I know what it is," she announced. "It's our next clue!"

ROLLIN' ON THE RIVER

"What kind of clue?" I asked.

"Listen," Ashley said. She shook the piece of silver, and it made a soft tinkling sound. "It's a bell! Hey, Jason! Check it out!"

"What's up?" Jason called as he ran back to us. He already had his life vest on.

I took the bell from Ashley and handed it to Jason. "Look familiar?" I asked.

Jason rolled the bell around in his hand. Then he nodded. "You bet! This is a bell from the missing drum. But how on earth did it end up on the riverbank?"

"We don't know yet," I said. "But it's a great clue."

I didn't bring my mini-tape recorder because I didn't want it to get wet. Luckily, Ashley still had her notebook. She wrote the word 'bell' under her list of clues.

Weasel looked over her shoulder as she wrote. "I don't think you two are such great detectives," he said. "You're just lucky. You found that bell only by accident."

"It's still a good clue," I told him. What was Weasel's problem, anyway?

I slipped the bell into my pocket as evidence. "And now we should look for some more clues."

When we got to the raft, Ashley and I put on life vests and helmets. Then Jason showed us how to use the wooden paddles.

"Be sure not to dig the paddles deep into the river," he told us. "Dip them just a few inches underwater."

The raft was the perfect size for four kids and a basset hound. Weasel sat in the back. Ashley and I sat in the middle. Jason sat up front with Clue.

"Let's go for it!" Weasel cried, as he pushed the raft into the water.

As the raft started floating, I called to Jason. "Why is the water so calm in some places? And like a bubble bath in others?"

"The water moves faster when it flows over rocks," Jason explained. "That's why the shallow water is usually choppy and the deep water is usually calm."

Just then Ashley and I got whacked with a huge splash of water. I gasped—I was soaking wet!

I spun around. Just as I thought. Weasel had splashed us with his paddle!

"Weasel, you creep!" Ashley cried.

But Weasel suddenly stopped smiling. His eyes grew wide. "White water coming up!" he shouted.

The raft began to move very fast. It swayed back and forth. Then it bounced over the rushing water.

"Should we paddle?" I shouted to Jason.

"Yeah," he called back. "But try not to hit the rocks!"

We bounced up and down. Every time the raft slammed into the river, water sprayed up into my face.

I heard Clue bark over the roar of the rapids.

"Get down, girl!" Ashley yelled. Clue lay down on the bottom of the raft.

"Watch out," Jason called. "Here comes the slope!"

"Slope?" I cried. "What slope?"

The river suddenly slanted like a slide. Our raft tumbled down about two feet of rushing water!

Ashley and I both screamed.

The raft settled and the water grew calm again. I took a deep breath. "Is it always like that?" I asked Jason.

"Why? Were you scared?" Weasel asked.

"A little," I admitted.

"Well, it's going to get worse," he said, giving me a nasty grin.

"What do you mean?" I asked.

Weasel didn't answer me. He just grinned that nasty grin again.

Ashley and I paddled along the river. We were having fun until Jason shouted, "Oh, no!"

He pointed up ahead. "There's a tree branch lying halfway across the river. We'll crash if we don't get our raft around it!"

"How do we do that?" Ashley asked.

"Paddle on the left side of the raft only," Jason ordered. "That ought to turn it around."

Since I was on the left side, I stuck my paddle into the river and began pulling it through the water. I paddled as fast as I could, but the raft didn't turn.

"We're going to hit the tree!" Ashley yelled.

I paddled even harder. The tree was only

about ten feet away.

"Come on!" Jason cried. He dragged his paddle through the water really fast. So did I.

Finally the raft began to turn. When we reached the fallen tree branch, the raft just barely floated past.

"We did it!" I shouted.

"Good work, crew!" Jason said.

Our raft jumped over some more white water, but it didn't seem scary anymore.

"This is better than a water park!" Ashley cried happily.

"You mean you're not scared?" Weasel asked. He sounded surprised. "You don't want to leave?"

I shook my head hard. "We'd never give up a case before we solved it."

But I couldn't help wondering—why did Weasel sound so disappointed that we weren't scared? Why did he want us to leave?

6

ASHLEY'S SURPRISE

We steered the raft over to the riverbank. Then we hopped out and dragged it to shore.

"I think Weasel is out to get us," I whispered to Ashley as we followed the boys into town.

"Why do you think that?" she whispered back.

"Because he kept asking us if we were scared on the river," I explained. "Plus, he told me our ride was going to get worse before Jason even saw that tree branch in the water."

"Maybe *he's* the thief," I continued. "Remember the note? It said our lives would be in danger if we stayed here. I think we'd better make Weasel Suspect Number Three."

"There's only one problem," Ashley said. "Weasel doesn't have a motive."

"You're right," I said. "Why would he steal Grandpa Joe's artifacts?"

Ashley pulled out her notebook and wrote "Weasel=Suspect #3. Maybe."

"Let's keep an eye on him," I said. I hurried to catch up with the boys.

We walked down a street lined with little shops. "I'd like to buy some things for Trent and Lizzie," I said.

Trent is our older brother. Lizzie is our little sister.

"Me, too," Ashley said. "But first we have to look for clues."

"Let's start questioning some of the people," I suggested. "Like that woman over there on the bench."

"Excuse me," I said as we walked over. "Did you notice anything strange last month on the night of the full moon?"

"Strange?" she repeated. "I don't think so. I can't even remember when the full moon was."

I heard Weasel snicker behind us.

Ashley smiled. "Thanks for your help," she said to the woman.

As we walked away, Weasel laughed. "Some detectives you are. Nobody is going to remember when the moon was full!"

"One person will remember," I said.

"Yeah," Ashley agreed. "The thief will remember, because he steals things only during the full moon."

"So if anyone remembers the full moon, we'll know they're the thief!" Jason said. "Great idea, Trenchcoat Twins!"

Weasel rolled his eyes. "This is stupid," he said. He stalked off down the street.

I gave a big sigh. "Thanks," I said.

"Who should we question next?" Ashley asked as we walked down the block.

I saw a man in a cowboy hat, standing in front of a small store. The sign on the window read SKIP'S SOUVENIR SHOP.

"That's Skip," Jason told us. "He owns the store."

Skip watched us closely as we walked over. "What can I do for you, kids?" he asked.

"We're wondering if you saw anything strange last time the moon was full," I told him.

Skip smiled. "My dog howled a whole lot more than usual, but that's about it," he said.

I glanced past Skip into his store.

"What kind of souvenirs do you have?" I asked.

"Just about anything you want!" Skip said quickly. "I even have a leash and a collar for your dog. It says 'Greetings from Montana' around the collar part."

I shook my head. "No, thanks. I—"

"I have a terrific clock!" Skip added. "It's shaped like a rooster, and every hour it yells cock-a-doodle—"

Jason grabbed my arm. "Thanks, Skip. But we don't have time to buy stuff today." We left Skip and walked around the corner.

"The souvenirs in Skip's store are bor-ring!" Jason explained. "Nobody ever shops in there."

"Then how does he stay in business?" Ashley asked.

Jason shrugged. "It's the only place in town where you can get keys made. And Skip isn't even very good at that. Last winter, we asked him to make a copy of the keys to the main house, and he made us a key that bent when we tried to use it!"

Ashley and I laughed.

Jason pointed to a big store at the end of the street. "Big Sky Treasures has all the neat souvenirs! Let's go there."

Jason was right. Big Sky Treasures had

hundreds of souvenirs from Montana. There were cowboy hats in every size and color. On practically every shelf was Native American jewelry and pottery. There was even a box filled with toy buffalo!

After we bought T-shirts for Trent and Lizzie, Ashley and I looked for souvenirs of our own. I bought a pair of silver eagle earrings. Ashley picked out a pair of beaded moccasins.

"We'd better head back to the ranch," Jason said as we left the store. "I promised Grandpa Joe I'd help with the cattle."

"And Mary-Kate and I should start looking for more clues," Ashley said. "Time is running out."

We walked back to the river. Ashley stepped into the raft—and let out a piercing scream!

"A snake!" she shrieked. "There's a snake in the raft!"

7

FINE-FEATHERED CLUE

Ashley jumped out of the raft. "The snake was right next to my foot!" she cried.

I held my breath and stared into the raft.

"It's...not moving," I said.

"That's because it's fake," Jason said. He reached down and grabbed the snake. "See?"

Jason was right. The snake was made out of rubber!

"You should have seen your faces!" Weasel laughed loudly.

"Mary-Kate!" Ashley said. She pointed to

the snake. "There's something hanging on the end. It looks like a note!"

I picked up the snake's tail and read the note. "It says, 'TRENCHCOAT TWINS, GO BACK TO CALIFORNIA—OR ELSE!'"

I felt my stomach flutter. The thief was warning us again.

"Hey, Weasel," Ashley said. "Where have you been? You weren't in Big Sky Treasures with us."

I grinned at Ashley. She was wondering the same thing I was—did Weasel put the snake and the note here?

"I was playing video games in the arcade," Weasel said. "I don't need any stupid souvenirs from Montana."

Weasel didn't sound as if he were lying. Maybe he didn't leave the note. But if it wasn't him, who was it?

We hardly said a word as we rafted back up the river. When we finally got back to the ranch, Ashley and I went to the display room to look for more clues.

"Mary-Kate?" Ashley asked. "The full moon is tomorrow night. What will we do if we don't find the thief by then?"

I thought for a moment. Then I snapped my fingers.

"We'll have a stakeout!" I exclaimed.

"A stakeout?" Ashley repeated.

I pointed out the door. "The living room is right across the hall. If we hide in there all night, we'll be able to see the thief when he sneaks into this room!"

Clue made a soft snuffling sound. She was sniffing the same corner of the rug over and over!

"What is she doing?" I asked. "There's nothing on the rug."

"Maybe there's something *under* the rug!" Ashley said.

We yanked up the corner of the rug. Ashley was right. There *was* something underneath— a long white feather!

"Way to go, Clue!" I cried.

Ashley picked up the feather. She twirled it between her fingers. "I wonder if this is a feather from the stolen headdress," she said.

"There's only one way to find out," I replied. I took the feather from Ashley and held it under Clue's nose. "Find the headdress, girl!"

Clue sneezed. Then she kicked up her feet and took off!

I pumped my fist in the air. "Ye-es!"

Clue dashed out of the main house and through the yard. Her long ears shot up as she leaped over the fence.

Ashley and I ran after Clue as she sped across a stretch of grass. We followed her through a herd of grazing cows. They all mooed at us.

"Where's Clue going?" Ashley called as we ran.

"She's heading for the ranch hands' houses!" I called back.

When she got to the little stretch of homes, Clue didn't even slow down. She ran straight up to a small yellow house. The door was open and Clue darted inside.

We chased Clue into the house. A red-haired girl stood in the living room. She looked about the same age as Ashley and I. She also looked pretty surprised.

"What's going on?" she asked.

Ashley and I didn't answer. We followed Clue out the back door into the yard. Clue stopped in front of a shed and barked.

"Ah-ha!" I cried. "The feathered headdress is probably inside that shed!"

"Can you please explain what's going on?" the girl asked again.

I grabbed the handle on the shed door.

"Sure," I told the girl. "But not until I do — *this*!"

I gave the door a good yank. It flew open.

"Mary-Kate!" Ashley cried. "Look out!"

8

DOGGONE DISASTER

*C*LANG! *CLUNK! CLINK!*

I covered my head as brooms, buckets, and feather dusters tumbled out of the shed!

"Great." The red-haired girl groaned. "Now look what you did!"

Clue plucked up a white feather duster. She shook it back and forth between her teeth.

"Good girl, Clue," Ashley said. She held the white feather against the feather duster. "It's a perfect match!"

"You mean the feather we found in the

main house belongs to a *feather duster*?" I asked. "How did that happen?"

"Easy," the girl said. "My mom is the ranch housekeeper. She cleans the main house twice a week."

"So that explains all the cleaning supplies in the shed," Ashley said.

The girl finally smiled. "I'm Lynn Keller. And I'll bet you two are the Trenchcoat Twins!"

I looked at the messy ground. I was so embarrassed!

"We're usually better detectives than this," I told her.

"At least your dog found a clue," Lynn said. "Even if it wasn't the one you really wanted."

Ashley sighed. "We're going to need a lot more clues before the full moon tomorrow night. That's when the thief will probably strike again."

"Wow!" Lynn said. "This is so exciting! What are you going to do next? Tell me! Tell me! Tell me!"

"We'd like to question as many people as we can," I explained. "But there isn't much time left."

Lynn's eyes lit up. "Why don't you come to the square dance tonight? Everyone will be there. You can question them all!"

"That's a great idea, Lynn," I said. "How can we thank you?"

Lynn pointed to the cleaning supplies on the ground. "You can start by helping me put all that junk back."

"Oh...no problem!" Ashley said quickly.

I looked down at the pile of dustpans, mops, and scrub brushes. How could *cleaning* supplies — be so *messy*?

That evening, Ashley and I followed Jason and Lynn to the ranch's recreation hall. We had decided to wear disguises so no one would know they were being watched by the Trenchcoat Twins.

I tucked my hair into a huge brown cowboy hat. My sweatshirt and pants were stuffed with pillows to make me look bigger. Lynn helped me paint freckles all over my face.

Ashley wore a red wig and dark sunglasses. She borrowed a scarf and a pair of dress-up high-heeled shoes from Lynn. Clue wore just a tiny cowboy hat. It's hard to disguise a dog!

"I feel like a glamorous movie star!" Ashley said.

I patted down my puffy stomach with both hands. "And I feel like a humongous marshmallow!" I groaned.

Jason opened the door of the rec hall. We stepped inside and looked around. "Wow," I said. "This looks like fun!"

There was a band onstage playing fiddles and guitars. People of all ages twirled on the dance floor. A table stood on the side, covered with plates and platters of delicious-looking food.

"Swing yer partner to the right!" a fiddler

with a cowboy hat sang. "Then twirl around with all yer might! Yeee-haaaa!"

Lynn pointed to the dance floor. "See? Everyone is here tonight. Even Emily and Henry Bixby."

"Look at their costumes!" Ashley giggled.

Henry was wearing a white cowboy suit with red and blue rhinestones. Emily wore a short, frilly yellow skirt and an orange blouse with huge, puffy sleeves.

"At least they're not stuffed with pillows!" I joked.

"I'll get us some fruit punch," Jason said.

"And I'll get a bowl of water for Clue," Lynn added.

Clue barked and followed them over to the snack table.

"Mary-Kate," Ashley whispered. "Weasel is coming this way!"

"Don't say anything to him," I whispered back. "Let's see if he recognizes us!"

Weasel walked up to me and Ashley. He

wore a black cowboy hat that was tipped way back on his head.

I held my breath as Weasel looked at me. Then he looked at Ashley—and he walked right by us.

"I'm out of here," he mumbled to himself. "These dances are bor-ring."

I watched Weasel leave the rec hall. Then I turned to Ashley. "I don't think he knew it was us, do you?" I asked. But Ashley was busy watching Henry and Emily on the dance floor.

"They really know how to square-dance," Ashley said.

Henry started spinning Emily so fast that her skirt flew out in a circle around her. When she finally stopped, something small peeked out of her skirt pocket.

"Look! It's their dog, Cinnamon," I said. "He must be dizzy."

I heard a bark from the other side of the rec hall. I knew that bark anywhere—it was Clue!

"Uh-oh," Ashley said.

"Clue, come back!" I called as Clue ran toward Cinnamon.

"Whose mutt is this?" Emily demanded.

Cinnamon growled down at Clue. Then he leaped out of Emily's pocket and chased Clue through the rec hall.

"Come on, Ashley," I cried. "We have to get Clue!"

"But we're supposed to be under cover," Ashley argued. "We don't want to draw attention to ourselves!"

I heard people shriek. Clue and Cinnamon ran through legs and jumped over feet.

"Cinnamon!" Emily called out. "Come to Mommy!"

"Clue!" I yelled. "Where are you?"

Woof! I spun around and saw Clue charging straight toward us. Cinnamon ran after her.

Henry stepped forward to grab Cinnamon—and he tripped over Clue!

"Arrrrrghhh!" he cried.

"Oh, no!" I groaned.

Henry hit the floor and something colorful flew out of his pocket. It soared through the air and landed in front of me with a clunk.

I looked at it and gasped.

"What is it, Mary-Kate?" Ashley asked.

"It looks like the stolen necklace!" I said.

9

HIDE...AND SNEAK!

"**L**et me see that!" Jason called from across the room.

I reached down to pick up the necklace. But before I could grab it, someone snatched it away!

It was Henry. He shoved the necklace into his jacket pocket.

"This spoils everything!" Henry mumbled as he, Emily, and Cinnamon stormed out of the rec hall.

"Was it the stolen necklace, Mary-Kate?"

Jason asked. "Could you tell?"

"How close did you look at it?" Ashley asked.

"Were the beads made of stone?" Lynn asked.

Everyone was talking at once. "Time out!" I called.

Ashley, Jason, and Lynn stared at me.

"All I know is that it *looked* like the stolen necklace," I said.

"Then we *have* to get a closer look," Ashley said.

"When?" Lynn asked.

"We can't do it now," Ashley said. "The necklace is in Henry's pocket. We'll have to wait until tomorrow."

"How can we get our hands on that necklace?" Jason asked. "We can't sneak into the Bixbys' guest house."

"I have an idea!" Ashley said. She turned to Lynn. "Maybe we can offer to clean the guest house, to help out your mom."

I nodded slowly. "I get it. And once we're inside, we can check out the necklace!"

"Mom will definitely let us do it," Lynn said. "She'll take all the help she can get!"

Jason looked disappointed. "I can't come. I help clean the barn every morning."

"That's okay, Jason," Ashley said. "We'll let you know what happens."

"Do you really think the Bixbys will let us *all* in to clean the house?" Ashley asked Lynn.

"Probably not," Lynn said. She leaned back in her chair and grinned. "Unless the two of you hide inside my mom's cleaning cart!"

"The *three* of us," I corrected her. "You forgot Clue!"

The next morning, Ashley and I checked out the cleaning cart in Lynn's backyard. Underneath was a built-in cabinet. On the top was a pile of cleaning supplies.

"You hide in the cabinet down there," Lynn said, pointing. "And I'll wheel it into the guest house."

"Can you push this thing with us in it?" Ashley asked.

"Are you kidding?" Lynn asked. She bent her arm to show her muscle. "No problem!"

I giggled. Ashley and I crawled inside the cabinet. Clue jumped in after us.

"Remember," Lynn warned. "Don't make any noise!"

Lynn slid the cabinet door shut. She left it open just a crack for air. It was pretty dark, but I could see a feather duster next to Clue. I hoped it wouldn't make her sneeze!

"Next stop, guest house!" Lynn called.

The cart began to roll. It bumped so much that Clue's ears flapped up and down. Ashley didn't look very comfy either.

At last it stopped. Ashley and I pressed our ears against the sides of the cart and listened. It sounded as if Lynn was knocking on a door.

"Good morning, Mr. Bixby," I heard Lynn say. "I've come to clean your guest house."

"Well, make it fast," Henry said. "It's Sunday

and my wife and I have things to do."

"Yeah, like steal another one of Grandpa Joe's treasures!" Ashley whispered.

The cart began to move and shake again. Then it came to a quick stop. I could hear Lynn talking to someone else.

"Shoo! Go away, Cinnamon!" she said.

"Oh, no," I whispered. "I forgot about Cinnamon."

I heard a soft snuffling noise. Cinnamon was smelling the cart. He was sniffing out Clue!

YAP! YAP! YAP! Cinnamon started to bark. *YAP! YAP! YAP!*

"Cinnamon?" Emily's voice called. "What's wrong?"

I pressed my eye to the crack in the door and stared out at the room. The first thing I saw was Emily's feet. She was standing right in front of us!

"Why is my dog barking at that cart?" Emily demanded. "Let me see what's inside."

I stared at Ashley in horror. We were caught!

10

EMILY COMES CLEAN

"**T**here's nothing in the cart!" Lynn told Emily. "Your dog probably smells my cat—she likes to sleep in there sometimes."

I crossed my fingers. Please let Emily believe her!

"I guess you're right," Emily finally said. "Well, you can start cleaning. I'll be in the bedroom, getting dressed."

I watched through the crack as Emily disappeared into the bedroom. Quickly, Lynn slid open the cart door. We climbed out into the

Bixbys' living room.

"Mr. Bixby left," Lynn told us. "But we have to search quickly. We have to finish by the time Mrs. Bixby is dressed."

"Okay, let's go!" I said. I stepped forward—and stopped.

Cinnamon stood right in front of us. He growled at Clue. Then he began to bark again!

"What's that racket?" Emily Bixby demanded.

I spun around. Mrs. Bixby stood in the doorway. And she was wearing the beaded necklace!

"All of you are here to clean?" Emily asked. She looked confused. "Are Henry and I that messy?"

I looked at the necklace again—and decided to get right to the point.

"We know that Henry stole the necklace you're wearing, Mrs. Bixby," I said.

"Stole?" Emily repeated. She touched the necklace. "Why would Henry steal? He can buy anything he wants."

"Except Mr. White Eagle's valuable necklace!" Ashley said.

"Henry *bought* this necklace for my birthday!" she insisted.

"Your birthday?" Lynn asked.

"It was yesterday," Emily said. "Henry was going to surprise me with the necklace at the square dance."

"Can we take a look at it?" I asked.

"Oh, I suppose so." Emily sighed. "But you're wasting your time. It's not Mr. White Eagle's missing necklace!"

Emily unhooked the necklace and gave it to me. I flipped it over in my hand. 'Brittany's of New York' was carved on the back of the biggest stone.

"What's Brittany's?" I asked Emily.

"Why, it's the most expensive jewelry store in the entire world!" Emily said. "I loved Mr. White Eagle's necklace so much, Henry had one made exactly like it."

Ashley and I looked at each other. Then I

handed the necklace back to Emily.

"Sorry for the mistake, Mrs. Bixby," I said.

"And happy birthday," Ashley added.

Ashley and I helped Lynn clean the Bixbys' guest house. Then we went back to the main house.

"This stinks," I told Ashley as we climbed the stairs to our room. "The full moon is just a few hours away, and we're nowhere!"

"Never give up," Ashley told me. "That's what Great-Grandma Olive always says."

We walked into our guest room—and froze. Weasel was standing right over Ashley's bed!

"What are *you* doing in here?" I cried.

Ashley gasped. "Mary-Kate! There's something on my pillow."

I ran over to Ashley's bed. There was a fake scorpion on the pillow and a note that said: TRENCHCOAT TWINS, GIVE UP!

I glared at Weasel.

"So it *was* you all the time," I said. "You're the thief!"

11

STAKEOUT!

"Thief? Me?" Weasel cried. "No way!"

"Why else would you leave us all those threatening notes unless you wanted us to go away?" Ashley demanded. "Because you didn't want to get caught!"

Weasel scrunched up his face. "I'm not the thief. But I did want you to leave. I was hoping you'd be so spooked by the notes that you'd go back to California."

"Why do you want us to leave?" Ashley asked.

"Because *I* wanted to solve this case!" Weasel said. "I know I could be a great detective if I had the chance. But all Jason kept talking about were the famous Trenchcoat Twins!"

"You should have told us you wanted to be a detective," I said.

Weasel sat down on the bed. "I thought you'd laugh at me," he admitted. "The kids around here always make fun of me for watching so many detective movies."

"We wouldn't make fun of you," I insisted.

"In fact, we'd probably ask you to help us!" Ashley added.

"But you already have a partner," Weasel said. He pointed to Clue. "That hound dog of yours!"

"Clue is a first-rate scent dog," I agreed. "But you're a first-rate *sneak*!"

"Yeah," Ashley said. "That can really come in handy when you're solving a mystery!"

"Hmm," Weasel said. "I guess I never thought about that."

I suddenly had a great idea!

"How would you like to help us stake out the living room tonight, Weasel?" I asked. "We still don't know who the thief is—and I think we've run out of clues. So this stakeout is very important. It's our last chance. Do you want to help?"

"You bet!" Weasel cried.

"But you have to promise not to play any more tricks on us!" Ashley said.

"Or tell us we're bad detectives!" I added.

Weasel nodded. "It's a deal!"

The door flew open and Jason and Lynn ran into the room.

"Lynn just told me that the Bixbys aren't the thieves," Jason said. "Now what?"

"We're having a stakeout tonight!" Weasel announced.

"Cool!" Jason cried.

"It'll be fun!" Lynn added.

"Wait a minute!" I said. "We can't all stake out the room."

"Sure we can, Mary-Kate," Ashley said. "This way, if one of us falls asleep, there'll be plenty of others still awake."

That was logical. Ashley was right, as usual!

"Okay," I said. "Let's make a plan."

Weasel grinned. "This is going to be the best stakeout in history!"

I held my mini-tape recorder to my mouth. "Ten-thirty P.M....Grandpa Joe and Mrs. White Eagle are up in their bedrooms. Crew stationed in living room...Let the stakeout begin!"

Weasel pumped his fist in the air.

Lynn giggled.

"Shhh!" Ashley whispered.

All the lights in the house were out. But the full moon was so bright that it lit up the whole room.

I glanced at the moon through the window. It was beautiful. But it also reminded me that this was our last chance.

"Doors locked?" I asked Jason.

"Check!" Jason said.

We huddled on the couch and peeked over the back. I could see the big wolf carving through the living room door.

"Can't we at least turn on the TV?" Lynn asked. "Or make popcorn? Or tell ghost stories?"

"This is a stakeout, Lynn," Ashley said. "We don't want the thief to hear us when he comes."

I whispered into my tape recorder again. "Ten thirty-five P.M....Stakeout in progress... Wolf carving in full view...all systems go!"

"I'm not tired," Jason said. "Are you tired, Weasel?"

"No way!" Weasel answered.

"Neither am I," Lynn said. "Are you, Ashley?"

"Nope," Ashley said. "I'm wide awake."

An hour later something white flew in through an open window.

"Hey, look," Weasel said. "It's a butterfly!"

"The butterfly is a symbol of sleep to the Blackfoot tribe," Jason said. He curled up in the corner of the couch and yawned.

Jason's yawn made me feel like yawning. But I held it back.

"Sleep, huh?" I asked. "That's...interesting."

"I never stayed up all night before," Lynn said. She leaned against the back of the couch and closed her eyes.

I glanced at Weasel. His eyes looked droopy.

The butterfly landed on Ashley's head. She brushed it off and yawned. Then I heard Jason begin to snore!

"Hey, you guys!" I whispered. "We can't all go to sleep...we have to..."

What did we have to do? I couldn't remember. I let my eyes close. I'll just take a short nap, I thought. Just for a few minutes....

WOOOOOO!

"Wh-what?" I gasped. I opened my eyes and

saw Clue. She was howling in my ear!

I suddenly had a horrible thought. I held my watch up to the moonlight. It was two-thirty in the morning!

"Oh, great!" I groaned. "Just great!"

I jumped up and ran across the hall. The full moon lit up the whole display room—and I could see that the wolf carving was gone.

I felt terrible. Jason was counting on Ashley and me to find the thief—and now the carving had been stolen right in front of us! "Some detectives we are," I said sadly.

I checked out the window. It was closed and locked. Nobody got in that way. Next I walked out to the front door of the house. It was locked, too. So was the back door.

Nobody broke into the house. But somehow the thief still got in and stole the wolf carving.

"We'll find the thief," I said out loud. "The wolf carving might be gone, but my detective skills aren't!"

12

STOP, THIEF!

I went into the living room and shook Ashley to wake her up.

"Mary-Kate? What's going on?" Ashley asked sleepily. Jason, Weasel, and Lynn woke up, too.

"The thief was here," I said. "He took the wolf."

"Oh, no." Jason groaned.

"Well, whoever he is, he could have wiped his feet," Lynn said. She pointed to the floor in the hallway. "What a slob!"

Footprints? Ashley and I ran over to see.

"They look muddy…and wet," I said.

"That's weird," Weasel said. "Most of the land around here is bone dry. And it hasn't rained in days!"

Ashley's mouth dropped open. "Hey…when we found the bell on the riverbank, it was muddy, too!"

"What are you saying, Ashley?" I asked.

"I'm saying that the thief might have come here by way of the Wild Wolf River!" Ashley said.

"At night?" Lynn asked doubtfully. "In the dark?"

"It's not *that* dark," I said. "Do you see how bright that moon is?"

Ashley stared at me. "Mary-Kate, that's it!" she cried. "That's why the thief steals only when the moon is full. So it's light enough to sneak the crafts away on a raft!"

"You're right," I said. "And if my hunch is right, we have to hurry—the thief is making his getaway on the river right now!"

"What are we waiting for?" Jason cried. "Let's go!"

As we ran toward the river, I thought about all the facts we had. I thought about the full moon, the muddy footprints, the locked windows and doors.

"That's it!" I exclaimed. "Ashley, the doors were *locked*. I know who the thief is!"

In the light of the full moon, I could see Ashley thinking. Then her face broke into a wide smile. "I know, too! Let's get him!"

"Look! He's paddling away!" Weasel pointed to a shadowy figure jumping into a raft.

Jason pointed to *his* raft. "Let's chase him," he said. "If the moon is enough light for him, it's light enough for us."

I took a deep breath. The river looked black and scary at night. But we had no choice.

"Let's go for it," I said. "We can't let him get away!"

13

BY THE LIGHT
OF THE MOON

We pulled on our helmets and life vests. Then we pushed the raft out into the river and jumped in.

We paddled fast and hard. The raft picked up speed as it bounced over the rushing white water.

"He's a lot closer now!" I shouted.

But then our raft jerked forward and came to a sudden stop.

"What happened?" Ashley asked.

Jason looked over the raft and sighed.

"We're stuck on a rock!"

"We have to do something!" I said.

Lynn pushed the tip of her paddle against the boulder.

"No, Lynn," Jason called. "Your paddle might break!"

"Do you have a better idea?" Lynn asked.

Jason nodded. "Rock from side to side!" he said.

"What?" I cried.

"Like this!" Weasel said. He leaned from right to left and back again.

We all did the same. But the raft didn't budge.

"Rock harder!" Jason ordered.

We rocked so hard that Clue's ears swung back and forth.

Suddenly the raft jerked. Then it glided off the rock.

"Yay!" I shouted. "We did it!"

"We are the *coolest*!" Weasel cheered.

"The best!" Lynn and Jason added.

"I just wish the thief would slow down!" Ashley said.

"It looks like he's going to *have* to!" Jason said. He pointed ahead. "His raft is headed straight for the fallen tree!"

I heard the thief's raft scrape against the tree trunk. His raft tipped and lurched. Then suddenly it bumped to a stop.

A dark figure flew out of the raft and into the water.

"He fell into the river!" Ashley cried.

"We have to save him!" I yelled.

"Help!" the thief shouted. He thrashed his arms over his head as the current dragged him away.

Jason cupped his hand around his mouth and yelled, "Keep your head and feet above the water. Move with the flow!"

But the rushing water was too loud for the thief to hear us.

"We've got to reach him!" I said.

We paddled like crazy until we were just a

few feet away from the thief. He was being pulled by the current so fast that I couldn't see his face.

Jason lifted a paddle and held it out to him.

"Grab on!" he shouted.

The thief reached out and took hold of the paddle. When he had a good grip, we all helped pull him into the raft.

"Steer over to the riverbank," Jason told us.

The thief lay facedown in the raft.

"Th-thanks for saving me, kids," he said. He sputtered and gasped for breath. Then he turned over on his back.

I looked down at the shivering thief. The full moon lit up his face. It was just who I thought it would be—the man from the boring souvenir shop.

"Skip!" Jason cried.

"I knew it was you!" I told Skip. "You stole the wolf carving."

"Did you also steal the other crafts?" Ashley asked.

Skip nodded. "But I had a good reason," he insisted. "Everyone was shopping at Big Sky Treasures for souvenirs. I needed those real Native American artifacts to bring in more customers!"

"You stole the crafts...and then you sold them?" I asked.

Skip shrugged. "What else could I do to compete?"

"You could have sold slushies!" Ashley cried.

When we reached the riverbank, Jason turned to me. "How did you know it was Skip?" he asked.

"Simple," I told him. "I checked out the doors and the windows, and I could tell that the thief hadn't broken into your house."

"So?" Jason asked, sounding confused.

"So the thief must have had keys to the house," I said.

Ashley nodded. "And you asked Skip to make copies of keys to the main house last winter," she said. "He must have made an extra copy for himself."

"Is that true?" Jason asked Skip.

Skip looked down. Then he nodded.

"What a horrible thing to do," Lynn said.

Skip sighed. "What I did was wrong—I know. But I'll make up for it. You have my promise!"

"Oh, yeah?" Jason asked. "How?"

"First thing tomorrow I'll contact all the people who bought the stolen crafts," Skip said. "Then I'll get them back for your grandpa Joe."

"Fair enough," Jason said. "But my grandpa Joe will still have to tell the sheriff."

"I suppose that's fair, too." Skip sighed. "If you help me get my raft off that tree branch, we can take your wolf carving home tonight."

Jason and Lynn took Skip back to his own raft. The wolf carving sat in the center of the raft.

Ashley and I stood with Weasel on the

riverbank and watched.

"Wow. Skip looks like he feels awful," Ashley said.

"Yeah. I think he does. But I can't wait to tell Grandpa Joe that he's getting his family treasures back," I said.

Ashley nodded. "And I can't wait to write in my notebook that this case is *finally solved*!"

We slapped a high-five.

For the first time since we got to the ranch, Weasel smiled at us—a nice smile, not a nasty one.

"I guess I'm not a very good detective, after all," he said.

"What do you mean?" I asked.

"Well, I had the two of you figured out all wrong," Weasel said. "You really *are* great detectives…even without your trenchcoats!"

Hi from both of us,

We couldn't believe the Bailey Brothers called us. Kyle, Theo, and Bobby Bailey are the hottest rock band around. But someone was playing dangerous tricks on them!

Ashley and I went undercover as rock singers to find out who was causing all the trouble. Was it rival group Simon and the Shooting Stars? A mysterious intruder? Or even Kyle Bailey!

Whoever it was, we had to find them fast, before the Baileys quit playing—forever!

Want to find out some more? Take a look at the sneak peek on the next page for The *New* Adventures of Mary-Kate & Ashley: The Case Of The Rock & Roll Mystery.

See you next time!

Love,
Ashley Olsen & Mary-Kate Olsen

· The Case Of The

Rock & Roll Mystery

Ashley put a hand on my shoulder. "Who's yelling?" she whispered.

"Sounds like someone is having a really bad fight," I answered. "We'd better go check it out."

"I think I'd better stay here and keep an eye out for Patty," Ashley told me. "Before she gets us into any more trouble. If we're not careful, everybody here will know we're undercover detectives."

Ashley peered into the shadows behind the stage. "It's really dark back there. You'd better be extra careful, Mary-Kate. Remember, we don't know who's behind all these 'accidents.' Whoever it is could turn out to be dangerous!"

I took my little tape recorder out of my

pocket and crept off into the darkness. The yelling was getting louder and louder. It sounded almost like...yes, it was! It was the Bailey Brothers. And they were having a big argument about something. I strained to hear them, but I couldn't quite make out their words.

"This could be really important," I thought. "I have to get closer!"

But I was afraid to move. The Bailey Brothers were standing in a little pool of light behind the curtains. I was sure they'd see me.

Then I had an idea. Maybe they wouldn't notice me on the floor. With my tape recorder clutched in one fist, I got down on my hands and knees and started to crawl forward on my stomach. Then I stopped.

I heard the sound of breathing right behind me!

I broke out in a cold sweat.

I was trapped in the shadows with a mysterious stranger!

Mary-Kate & Ashley
Ready for Fun and Adventure? Read All Our Books!

THE NEW ADVENTURES OF MARY-KATE & ASHLEY™

- ☐ BBO-0-590-29542-X   The Case of the Ballet Bandit $3.99
- ☐ BBO-0-590-29307-9   The Case of 202 Clues $3.99
- ☐ BBO-0-590-29305-5   The Case of the Blue-Ribbon Horse $3.99
- ☐ BBO-0-590-29397-4   The Case of the Haunted Camp $3.99
- ☐ BBO-0-590-29401-6   The Case of the Wild Wolf River $3.99
- ☐ BBO-0-590-29402-4   The Case of the Rock & Roll Mystery $3.99
- ☐ BBO-0-590-29404-0   The Case of the Missing Mummy $3.99
- ☐ BBO-0-590-29403-2   The Case of the Surprise Call $3.99
- ☐ BBO-0-439-06043-5   The Case of the Disappearing Princess $3.99

THE ADVENTURES OF MARY-KATE & ASHLEY™

- ☐ BBO-0-590-86369-X   The Case of the Sea World™ Adventure $3.99
- ☐ BBO-0-590-86370-3   The Case of the Mystery Cruise $3.99
- ☐ BBO-0-590-86231-6   The Case of the Funhouse Mystery $3.99
- ☐ BBO-0-590-88008-X   The Case of the U.S. Space Camp™ Mission $3.99
- ☐ BBO-0-590-88009-8   The Case of the Christmas Caper $3.99
- ☐ BBO-0-590-88010-1   The Case of the Shark Encounter $3.99
- ☐ BBO-0-590-88013-6   The Case of the Hotel Who-Done-It $3.99
- ☐ BBO-0-590-88014-4   The Case of the Volcano Mystery $3.99
- ☐ BBO-0-590-88015-2   The Case of the U.S. Navy Adventure $3.99
- ☐ BBO-0-590-88016-0   The Case of Thorn Mansion $3.99

YOU'RE INVITED TO MARY-KATE & ASHLEY'S™

- ☐ BBO-0-590-76958-8   You're Invited to Mary-Kate & Ashley's Christmas Party $12.95
- ☐ BBO-0-590-88012-8   You're Invited to Mary-Kate & Ashley's Hawaiian Beach Party $12.95
- ☐ BBO-0-590-88007-1   You're Invited to Mary-Kate & Ashley's Sleepover Party $12.95
- ☐ BBO-0-590-22593-6   You're Invited to Mary-Kate & Ashley's Birthday Party $12.95
- ☐ BBO-0-590-29399-0   You're Invited to Mary-Kate & Ashley's Ballet Party $12.95

- -

Available wherever you buy books, or use this order form
SCHOLASTIC INC., P.O. Box 7502, 2931 East McCarty Street, Jefferson City, MO 65102

Please send me the books I have checked above. I am enclosing $_____ (please add $2.00 to cover shipping and handling). Send check or money order—no cash or C.O.D.s please.

Name _____

Address _____

City_____ State/Zip_____

Please allow four to six weeks for delivery. Offer good in the U.S.A. only. Sorry, mail orders are not available to residents of Canada. Prices subject to change.

The Adventures of MARY-KATE & ASHLEY™

Look for the best-selling detective home video episodes.

The Case Of The Volcano Adventure™
The Case Of The U.S. Navy Mystery™
The Case Of The Hotel Who•Done•It™
The Case Of The Shark Encounter™
The Case Of The U.S. Space Camp® Mission™
The Case Of The Fun House Mystery™
The Case Of The Christmas Caper™
The Case Of The Sea World® Adventure™
The Case Of The Mystery Cruise™
The Case Of The Logical i Ranch™
The Case Of Thorn Mansion™

Join the fun!

You're Invited To Mary-Kate & Ashley's™ Costume Party™ NEW
You're Invited To Mary-Kate & Ashley's™ Mall Party™ NEW
You're Invited To Mary-Kate & Ashley's™ Camp Out Party™
You're Invited To Mary-Kate & Ashley's™ Ballet Party™
You're Invited To Mary-Kate & Ashley's™ Birthday Party™
You're Invited To Mary-Kate & Ashley's™ Christmas Party™
You're Invited To Mary-Kate & Ashley's™ Sleepover Party™
You're Invited To Mary-Kate & Ashley's™ Hawaiian Beach Party™

And also available:
Mary-Kate and Ashley Olsen: Our Music Video™
Mary-Kate and Ashley Olsen: Our First Video™

DUALSTAR
VIDEO

Don't Miss

Mary-Kate & Ashley

in their 2 newest videos!

Available Now Only on Video.